Let's Go 'Noles!

Aimee Aryal

Illustrated by Krystal Higgins

www.mascotbooks.com

It was a beautiful fall day at
Florida State University.

Two little Seminole fans were on
their way to Doak Campbell Stadium
to watch a football game.

The little fans passed by dorms
and classroom buildings.
They walked down Landis Green.

A professor passing by said,
"Let's Go 'Noles!"

The little fans stopped in front
of Strozier Library.

A librarian coming out of the building
waved and said, "Let's Go 'Noles!"

The little fans walked to
Oglesby Union.

Some students studying in the courtyard
said, "Let's Go 'Noles!"

The little fans went over to the
Civic Center where the Seminoles
play basketball.

A group of FSU fans standing outside
shouted, "Let's Go 'Noles!"

It was almost time for the football game.
As the little fans walked to the stadium,
they passed by some alumni.

The alumni remembered going
to games when they went to FSU.
They yelled, "Let's Go 'Noles!"

Finally, the little fans arrived at the
stadium. They watched Chief Osceola
ride his horse, Renegade, onto the field.

The little fans and the crowd made a chopping motion with their arms and shouted the FSU "War Chant."

The little fans watched the game from the stands and cheered for the team.

The Seminoles scored six points!
The quarterback yelled,
"Touchdown 'Noles!"

At half-time the Marching Chiefs
performed on the field.

The little fans watched the band
and listened to the "FSU Fight Song."

The Florida State Seminoles
won the football game!

The little fans gave Coach Bowden a
high-five. The coach said,
"Great game 'Noles!"

After the football game, the little fans
were tired. It had been a long day at
Florida State University.

They walked to their homes
and climbed into their beds.

"Goodnight little Seminole fans."

For Anna and Maya; Sophia, Olivia and Isabella;
and all little Seminole fans. ~ AA

To my California monkeys:
Josh, Mike and Miller. ~ KH

Special thanks to:

Bobby Bowden

Sherri Dye

For information please contact Mascot Books,
P.O. Box 220157, Chantilly, VA 20153-0157.

FLORIDA STATE UNIVERSITY, FLORIDA STATE, FSU, SEMINOLES, 'NOLES, FLORIDA STATE SEMINOLES,
and FSU SEMINOLES are trademarks or registered trademarks of Florida State University
and are used under license.

ISBN: 1-932888-20-9

Printed in the United States.

www.mascotbooks.com